john
URBANCIK

ANNABEL LEE,
in shadow

john URBANCIK

ANNABEL LEE, IN SHADOW

For more information, please visit www.darkfluidity.com

ISBN: 978-1-951522-11-7

ANNABEL LEE, IN SHADOW

I've walked a long time
through the shadows,
    those other worlds
       where nightmares
       persist,
    those other people
       whose grins hide
       sharp teeth.

I never really believed
    the shadows
    feared me.

I didn't know
    what I brought.

My tears left
    a path of gold
    inevitably
    leading to me.

And the things we fear,
    we often try to destroy.

These are snapshots
    of my nights
    in shadows.

I never believed
I was invincible.

I believe it less now.

I wore through
my feet
and burned through
several pairs of eyes.

My burdens
weighed me down
and the man
pursuing me
got closer
every day.

The man
from the shadows
mirrored me
in every way.
He stole
my ways of speaking,
my gate,
my scent,
and my breath.
He looked like me
but he wasn't.
He reflected
My worst parts,
my failures externalized,
my struggles made flesh.
He laughed
without joy
and whispered promises
as I slept
so he could erode
my sense of reality
and my sense of self.

She speaks in all languages
but mine
because she needs
no words
to tell me
her intentions.

Her blade is sharp
and still wet
from her last kill.

I tell her no
in a hundred languages.
She laughs at me
and grins,
but she doesn't stick me
with her blade.

Not this night.

She blows me a kiss,
a promise
we'll meet again.

She wanted me
  to know
  things I couldn't
            shouldn't
            wouldn't
                know,
    not under any
      normal circumstance,
    not in any
      normal place.
She taught me
  and I studied
    every word she said
    and every inch of her flesh
      until all her secrets
      were mine
      and mine alone.
Then she faded away,
  having given me
  everything
    knowing
    the shadows
    would consume
    her empty husk.

Winter announces itself
with a blaze of snow
reflecting the shadows
with stark objectivity.

I watch the shadows
from within them,
where they cannot escape
my constant attention.

They send distractions,
lithe supple shadows
overflowing with feminine curves
but no more substantial
than any other shadow.

Their masquerade
is shallow and thin,
but I play along
wishing for even
the hint of a thrill.

Walking alone
in shadows,
after days
and months
you start to see
the shapes of figures
    watching
    stalking
    craving
        the taste of your flesh,
and you start to think
maybe it wouldn't be so bad
just this one time,
the brief contact
like a balm,
but you'll never
never
wash the taste
from your mouth.

I fight against it,
but slowly
I am becoming
the monsters
I've been fleeing
and fighting.
I resist,
but I find cruelty
even if it brings me
no joy.
It's a survival mechanism,
or so I convince myself.
But I'm a liar
and I'm so ready
to believe.

Darkness falls.
The Moon
rises
and so do I.

Slowly,
you learn your talents
and transform them
into skills
by practice
and repetition.

I never expected
to find
a talent for knives,
a propensity for poisons,
but when circumstances
force you
to excel or die,
sometimes you're able,
no matter how,
to make the best
of a bad situation.

As I made my way
through the shadow realms,
I found
the shadows
already knew me.

New York.
I don't remember
the year.
I step back and forth
and sideways
through time.
In the shadow
of the Empire State Building,
I was caught
by a woman
more ethereal than I
ever could be.
She taught me things,
then extracted
my knowledge and history,
thinking she'd leave
a desiccated husk,
but I was
more resilient
than either of us
expected.

The man from
the shadows
preceded me
to every inn
and tavern
with tales
of my conquests,
the blood spilt
in my name
and by my hand.
Not all the stories
were true,
but when there are
no survivors,
there's no one
to put truth
to the stories.

Spend enough time
   in the shadows,
   you start to see them
   everywhere,
     in every bar,
     on every corner,
   riding the bus
     and the metro.
   You recognize them
     in libraries
     and bookstores,
     supermarkets,
     playgrounds
       and parks.
You see the shadows
even under
the brightest
sunlight.

More than once,
I thought this was it,
I couldn't go on anymore,
my body has limits
and I've surpassed them.
But always,
I found strength
for another step,
stamina to take another punch,
sheer anger or frustration enough
to throw my own.
Without exception,
not even when I cracked my ribs
and broke my foot,
I found the limits
I suspected for my body
were all in my head.

I thought
continuing to survive
and even thrive
under these
circumstances
meant I was winning,
but I was becoming
one of the shadows
myself,
and the shadows
are anonymous.
So I resisted this, too,
and asked the woman
of languages
for her name.
She struggled to answer,
but I was persistent
until finally she said,
Annabel Lee.
She stole the name,
but it made her unique
in the shadows,
and I told her
mine.

Whole cities rose
in the shadows,
providing sanctuary
to the lost
and wounded souls
cast so mercilessly
out of the light.
Souls like mine.

Once upon a time,
I wasn't feared,
I didn't inspire
tremors and shaking,
I didn't cause men
and women alike
to run,
to hide,
to flee deeper into shadows.

I'm sinking deeper
into shadow cities
where nothing you see
is real,
not even
the illusions.

The angle of the sun
changes the intensity
of the shadows.
At dusk,
I get excitable.
My heartrate increases.
My vision runs red.
My fists close tight.
But I repress
my rage
and wait
for the right target.
The man from the shadows
looks like me
and sounds like me,
but he doesn't show.

I wander the streets
and alleys
and rundown bars
but I won't find
the man from the shadows
anywhere
in this city.
The whiskey helps,
but the women taunt me
and laugh at me,
inadvertently
leading me
straight
to him.
He smiles
and shrugs
inside
my mirror
because he wears my face
but I
will
expose
him.

She tells me secrets.
Some are hers to tell.
I don't know which.
She feeds me bourbon
and bad ideas,
and I think
she likes
when I get into fights.
She enjoys
tending to my
bruised knuckles
after putting down
a man who wronged her.
There are so many.
Too many.
But she gives
my anger
focus.

A child snuck
into the shadows
to get a taste
of what was to come.
I told him
it couldn't be
all darkness,
he was too young
to be so ruined.
He told me
we all have a secret
that's ours to learn
and ours to keep.
He said
I was looking
too hard
for something
locked away
inside me.

The man from the shadows
offers a truce.
He'll change his face,
his voice, his name,
if I accept him
as an equal.
It's a trick.
He'll keep my face,
voice, and name
until the shadows
crumble to dust
like mountains.

She and I
steal moments
from the dark.
We tell each other jokes,
and even when they're bad,
we laugh.
We eat ice cream together.
We waltz
under the new moon
when the shadows
are at their weakest.
She draws strength
from me,
and I from her,
else otherwise
maybe
the shadows
would win.

No matter how strong,
how sneaky,
how confident,
I'm not enough
to face all my enemies
at once.

In a city of shadows,
they corner me,
they overwhelm me,
and they hurt me.

Again and again.

The man from the shadows
fights beside me.
The others
don't know the difference.
And if I fall,
who will he torment?

I withstood it all
until I saw
the face of Annabel Lee
among my opponents.

How deep
into a shadow city
can you descend
to escape your demons
when the one who broke you
insists on hiding
with you?

I can be your comfort.
Your solace.
Your joy.

She says this through
sharp teeth
and a tongue
tinged with poison.
But still,
I let her kiss me.

She says
you must be broken
to your component pieces,
ripped apart,
reduced to ash
and the memory
of a breath.
Cut down
at the knees,
blinded,
cracked,
hopeless and helpless.
Only then
can I re-make you
into the man
I want you
to be.
I desperately
want to believe her.
Instead,
I fight.
My nature
doesn't change.

Has it been days,
weeks, or months?
Time loses meaning
in places of shadow,
and I am burrowing
into the deepest
of them.
When I finally find
a place I think
will suffice,
Annabel Lee
is there
waiting for me.

She says,
  "I have been beaten
  and hidden away,
  used in every
  possible way,
  ruined,
  and ultimately
  destroyed.
  But you gave me hope.
  You gave me pleasure.
  Reason to fight
  to live.
  I owe you
  everything."

It's more
than I can take.
Lacking words,
I cry.

The man from the shadows
finds me at my lowest
to laugh.
She lies, he tells me,
but it's not true.
He's mistaken.
Lies require intention.
Promises require the same.
It's not a lie
if she's wrong.
It's a mistake.
A forgivable transgression,
not another betrayal.
The man from the shadows
laughs
and walks away
and turns out
the light.

No shadows
remain
quiet or still.
They all come
to see
the spectacle
they've made
of me.
Their fists
are darkened
by my blood,
already dry,
and they
taunt me
with the body
of Annabel Lee
as finally
they transform her
from beauty
and grace
misplaced
into a corpse.

Rage blinds me.
I have been stuck
in the shadows
so long,
I am one
of them,
so when I
crunch my fists
they feel it
and do not recover
easily.
In this way,
I exhaust myself.
When I wake,
I find dead shadows,
destroyed and mutilated
and unbreathing.
So many of them.
Now only their ghosts
can haunt me.
And this city of shadows
belongs to me.

I see her shadow,
the shadow of her shadow,
in the corner of my eye,
but when I turn to look,
I am alone.

The man from the shadows,
from the mirrors,
from the surface
of a lake
I barely remember,
clings to me
like I'm salvation,
and I know
I'll never see him again.
He's purged me,
or I've purged him,
and we part
to become strangers
and echoing memories.

I thought
I'd lost her
forever,
but she was
a shadow,
and shadows
never die.

LA DIOSA
DEL FUEGO

A goddess of fire
came to tease and tempt me
one night
while the moon was full
and the jazz soft
and transportative.
She threatened me
with poisons
and when she touched me
with just the tip
of her fingers,
I burned
inside and out.
Now my dreams
cannot be sated,
as I would dance
with a goddess of fire
and let the world burn.

Eight thousand miles away
across vast oceans
and whole continents,
my fiery goddess waits,
but does she wait for me
with open arms
and lingering kisses
or burning fingertips
and vengeance
against the past wrongs
of others who tried
to love her
before me?

I cross an ocean
bringing gifts
for a goddess of fire
and a question.
I will ask
if she'd dance with me.
A slow, quiet dance
under the light
of the moon
that maybe lasts
all through the night.
I would feel
the fire in her veins
and she would taste
my breath
on her throat
and I can dream
of where
she might take me
tomorrow.

My goddess of fire
will dance
until storms
swirl overhead.
Her rhythms
will break the sky
and bring the thunder.
She will dance
as the shredded remains
of my heart
are scattered
by the winds.
An explosion of lightning
might return me
to life,
but my goddess of fire
will already
have forgotten me
and the beautiful storms
we made together
when we danced.

I fell in love
with a goddess
of fire
and she burned me
to ash.

Her kisses
can soothe me
to the bone
or burn me up
from the inside.

She demanded gifts
but I was a fool.
I tried to give
a goddess of fire
something hot
and intangible,
but she took it
and laughed.

I tried to give
a goddess of fire
something cold and icy
but it withered
instantly
in her hands.

I tried to give
a goddess of fire
the gift of me,
wrapped up in a bow,
but she said
I was already hers.

She demands gifts,
and all I have
are words.

I drown in her flames
which I eagerly consume.

A goddess of fire
asked me to dance.
She sang to me
and whispered secrets
and held me close.
In a fever,
blood boiling,
heart pounding,
I agreed
to the dance
and she took
my heart
in her teeth
as a prize.

She dances
when I'm not there.
She sings
songs to me
in my sleep.
She whispers
with hot breath
against my ear
in the middle
of darkness.
She burns
with all the fires
of every volcano
and claims
she burns for me
and me alone.
But she is a goddess
and I am enthralled
and I don't care
if she doesn't love me
when she loves me.

She whispers,
which you wouldn't expect,
and entices
you to dance.
She'll flail her arms
and take an eye.
She'll flail her arms
and take your heart
but she consumes it
blood red rare.

If she's got a secret,
she doesn't keep it long.
She burns through
all that's hidden
until it's revealed,
broiled,
and skewered.
What she wants now,
she may
or may not
want tomorrow.
A goddess of fire
forgets the things
she once wanted
when a new desire
burns in her heart.

Dance with me,
the goddess of fire
demands,
and what choice is there
but to dance
even as you feel your heart
being roasted
on a spit?

Maybe it can't last forever,
but while it does
the goddess of fire
loves you
like no one ever has,
will, or can.
Even when your heart
is charred and shredded
in your chest,
you will count yourself lucky,
always wishing
for one more day.

I will search
for a goddess of fire
down rivers
over mountains
to the deepest depths
of the ocean.
When I find her
she will laugh
because I didn't
come first
to her volcano,
but the road
from where I started
to where she reigns
is long, arduous,
and filled with danger.
So, too, is the road back,
which she'll set me on
all on my own,
but I don't think
I can go back
to where I started.

In the cold
of night
she comes to me
bringing gifts of fire
to burn into my soul
and claim me
and never let me go,
but in the morning
the sun rises again
and she forgets,
she moves on,
she forges new steel
on faraway shores
and maybe sometimes
but not always
finds me again
when I need
her fire.

She dances
she teases
she tempts
and she lures me
wherever
she wants to go.

I'm easy
because
I'm willing,
and my soul's
been broken already.
What more
can she do?

But she kisses me
in moonlight
and solders
the fragments
of my heart
until they resemble
something
mechanical
but infused
with the rhythm
of her dance.

Musicians bring
their instruments
to tempt my
goddess of fire
to grant their wishes
and heal their wounds.
This night,
she is mine
(or I am hers)
and the players
merely change
the tempo
of the dance.
She uses me,
adores me,
grants my wishes,
and heals my wounds
before burning me out
and leaving me
ashen-faced and alone
to watch
the rising sun.

She burns through me,
leaving only cooling cinders
and cold ash,
then encourages me
to dance again,
to embrace the moonlight,
to listen to the drums
and lose myself
in their rhythm
until I am born
or re-born
into the night,
into her arms,
into one final kiss
before she leaves me
fresh and raw
and new.

It's love,
if just for
tonight,
to the rhythm
of the drums.
The fire
burns away
parts of me
I no longer need.
The goddess dances
for her own pleasure,
not just mine.
She takes me
and takes from me,
scraping down
to the bones,
so when it's over
and she's moved on,
I'm left to rise
to the rhythm
of distant drums
from my own ashes.

Abandoned
by my goddess of fire,
I dance alone
through cool ash
and gentle breezes
in search of
any
tiny
spark.

ROMANCE
AND
MISCELLANY

I might
say you're beautiful,
but you should realize
I see you
as you were,
as you are,
and as you will be.
I see beyond the skin,
beyond the glamour,
beyond just the color
of your eyes and lips.
When I say it,
I mean it thoroughly
and completely,
deeply and broadly.
You are beautiful.

Two thousand miles
don't mean anything
when I can look
at the moon
and see your eyes
looking back,
when I can
run my fingers
through the thin smoke
wafting from that candle
and know you can feel
my fingers tracing
the small of your back.
Yet I feel
every mile
when I want
to share your breath.
What magic
can bring us together?

A creature of
indescribable beauty,
she is,
drawing every eye
and inciting
whispered hopes
and dreams
already crashed.
She walks
or glides
or floats,
and she talks
quietly
on a cell phone,
but I'm close enough
to hear the words
and see the
exasperation
in her eyes.
She knows I hear them,
so I give her
a weak smile
and look away.
She'd said,
"They're staring at me
again."

His face isn't weathered.
It's the world
that's cracked at the edges.
His voice is as deep and strong
as ever,
but the atmosphere
has thinned
and cannot carry
the weight of his words.
All of reality,
he comes to accept,
runs on clockworks,
and no one's been oiling the gears.
It's not his bones
under his skin
that creak,
it's the bones of a world
running dry.

Who are you to me
and how did it happen
that my every action
and every thought
are meant to impress you
by not trying to impress you?
This is some strange magic
or maybe I just don't
have tolerance left
for foolishness.
Yet I am thoroughly
enchanted
and I doubt you did anything
to make this happen.
You merely allowed it,
and here I am
eager to accept
any version of our future.

You speak to me
without need of words
and touch my soul
gently
because you know
it has been broken
like my heart,
and like my heart,
you know
it can be healed.

You have
infected me
with the poison
of your kiss
and the touch
of your hand
and the nearness
of your breath
to my throat.
Now you're in my head
and you're in my heart
and all my dreams
have your shape.

Are we more now
than we were
yesterday?
You'd already
awakened
my hunger.
The flames
had been lit.
But now
they're
stoked
and driven
to higher heights
and deeper depths
and hotter temperatures.
I will dream
of things
we haven't yet done.

If I touch you
again
I might lose
all control.
I've lost my heart already,
my mind, my essence.
If I taste
your lips
one more time,
I will never
want to stop.

You've infected my dreams
already,
then you say something
that changes the course
of tonight's dreams,
not just the long term ones.
I can't get away from you
even when you're not near,
and I'm not trying to.
get away.

I have seen
your darkness,
tasted
your desperation,
and felt
your heart race.
I am aware
of your flaws,
the challenges
you face daily,
and how you might
filet my heart
still beating
for you,
but my love
grows only deeper,
so when I next
hold your heart
in my hands,
trust
that I know
how precious
it is.

You know
I want you,
my heart burns
like a thousand suns.
You know
I love you,
I listen and I see
and I understand.
But do you know
I consider
your heart
a fragile jewel,
invaluable
but vulnerable
like mine;
and I consider
your kiss
the fuel of dreams;
and I consider
your body
a feast
for my ravenous soul;
and I consider
you—the essence of you—
a gift
worthy of gods
even when you offer
you to me?

Every breath we share,
  every thought
  and dream
  and vision
  and kiss,
  every conversation
    real
    imagined
    feared,
  every touch
    even when not
    physical,
  brings us closer
    to who we are
    supposed to be
    and who we are
    and who we've
      always been.
So kiss me
  again
or talk with me
or dream of me
or let me dream
  of you.

Thunder cracks the sky open
and all the rain
pours down on us
holding hands
and smiling
and holding hearts
close to each other
awaiting the next flash
of lightning,
the next boom
of thunder,
the next beat
of two hearts
in perfect unison.

You are invited
to be inappropriate.
It's just a weekend
or maybe more.
We can figure that out later
if our dreams
coalesce
and our hearts
find complimentary rhythms.
It might be
our first kiss
later
in some private moment,
but it doesn't
have to be the last
and it's okay
if it doesn't happen at all.
You held me
briefly
like it mattered,
and I will keep that
with me
forever.

I think I'm flirting.
I'm terrible at this.
I don't know where to start
or where to stop.
I never know
if I'm saying
or doing
the right thing.
And if you're flirting, too,
I am probably stupid enough
to believe you don't mean it.

She crushes dried rose petals
   plucked weeks ago
      into the mixture,
   then whispers my name
      to the moon.
She sends shadows
   to retrieve me,
   to kidnap me,
      but it's a wasted effort.
I would've come
   crawling
      if she'd asked.

How about a dream together?
We can go anywhere
at any time.
Paris in the 20s.
An empty beach
before there was anyone
to interrupt us.
We can talk about whatever
and dance under the moon
and kiss for days on end.
There's much to explore
and all the time
that's ever been
if we do it
in a dream
we share.

A dream,
a vision:
I'm not sure
what you are
just yet.

I'm going to dream
tonight
of forbidden things
because you've
encouraged me
to think
forbidden thoughts.

Under the moon's light
we dance a slow dance
and briefly,
you touch my lips
with your finger
and show me
the graves
of previous lovers
beneath us.

Let me in
to sit with you
in your darkness
and your silence
until you're ready
to share your burdens.
Then we can dance
under fresh moonbeams
and dream
new lives
into existence.

It's quiet now
as long as you
avoid the shadows,
unless you want
those chittering things
nibbling on your flesh,
your bones,
your soul.
When you start
screaming,
you'll attract more attention
and they'll swarm
over you
like a southern
barbeque
and I'll meet
one of them later
in an alley
gnawing on your femur
trying to make
a deal.

That's
not
the kind of
penny
we play
for
here.

I know you're broken.
We're all broken.
That doesn't mean
we need fixing.
Beauty is often broken,
and your beauty from inside
shines when you give it a chance.
You showed me that
the night you cried
for the ways in which I am broken.

You don't love me.
You just love being loved.

I dreamt
long ago
of someone
like you.
Beautiful.
Powerful.
Lovely
in every way.
I never
imagined
you would steal
my breath
and then my heart
with just
a single kiss.

I'm not too insecure
to climb onto the back
of your Harley,
wrap my arms around
your waist,
feel every cubic inch
vibrating through our bodies
as you take me
wherever you'll take me.

There's a breath
that needs taking.
I'll take it
with you.

My tale cannot be told
    except in whispers
    and only by the bravest
    and strongest
    and truest of heart.
And it can only be heard
    and understood
    by someone
    like you.

But lean in close
    and I will tell you
    from beginning to end
    the songs sung
    and yet to be heard.
I will answer
    your questions,
    reveal all your secrets,
    and show you how
    the story of me
    is the story of you.

Do you know how cold it's been
since you've gone?
The nights stretch
like there's no end,
and the stars throw ice
that cuts through flesh
and bone.
And I'm supposed to
pretend like I'm okay,
like the chill doesn't wreck me
fresh every night?
Do you know how cold it's been
when I can't even bear
to feel my own heart beat
in a ribcage of frost?

How much strength
will I need
tomorrow,
when you still
aren't here?

The last time we kissed,
we nearly burned
the whole fucking city down.
And now you want to dance?
I'm in.

I remember
the walks through parks,
over bridges,
in the Parisian rain.

I remember driving
on interstates with strange numbers,
along rivers and cliffs,
to cities unimagined.

I remember holding your hand,
and touching your lips
and whispering secrets
we'd never share again.

I remember my last breath
before your last breath,
and how much it hurt
to take the next.

A sordid start
  an impossible future
    dreams and nightmares
     and terrific fancies.
  Promises unspoken
   but made
    just the same.
All the dangers
  ingested
  digested
  regurgitated
   until there's nothing
    remaining
     but new emotions
      raw and unfelt
      since the dawn of time.
A dangerous path
  but the only one
   worth walking.

Some of the words
    are stories,
    explorations
        not of what
        I've done
        but the ways
        I've felt.
So when you
    see yourself
    in my words
        though you know
        we've never danced
        in the moonlight
        of Eldorado,
    know the words
        are stories
    but the emotions
        are true,
            then come with me
            to a café
            where we can watch
            the aurora
                burn the sky.

And even us, even here
in the coldest corners
of a galaxy
absurd in its miniscule size,
where the cosmic winds
barely tickle the stars,
where we have been forgotten
and neglected for a billion years;
even us, for whom hearts
dance under the rhythms
of feet, for whom lips
taste the sweetest atoms,
the universe pulses and spins
and draws unnecessary breath;
even fleeing our own worst sins,
we might again find each other.
Even us.
Even here.

You whispered to me
once
and I remember.
Not the words,
not even the meaning,
nor your intent
with your lips
so close to my ear.
I remember the touch
of your breath on my skin,
the goosebumps,
the warmth,
and the cold
when you went away.
You whispered to me
once
but the storm
you shared
direct in my ear
has gone still.
All that remains
is my storm raging
at your absence.

Forgotten
  are the lies
    we shared
  the scars
  the screams
    cutting the shallows
      of who we were.
Lost
  are the memories
  the places
  the people
  the dreams
    of the distant victories
    of who we might be.
Imperfect,
  we must be,
  but perfect
  in our shared
    bloodletting.

Did you get
what you want
from me?
Then go.
I don't need you
still hanging around
picking at my bones
with your long, dirty
fingernails,
no matter how sharp.

You know I love you
but I'm not allowed
to say these words.
You'll panic again,
and send me away.

Ghosts whisper
in the dark
trying to convince you
the things you saw
never happened
and the things you heard
were never said.
They lie.
Don't trust them.

A ghost in the eyes,
  maybe she's real
  maybe she's only
    for you
  with her razorblade
    fingernails
  and bloodshot eyes,
  skin that looks
    like gossamer
    but cuts.
And the words
  she says,
  the stories she shares,
  of hellish highways
  and scimitars
  and roses,
    they leave echoes
    in your ears
    that will haunt you.

Will we dance,
you and me,
witnessed by the moon?
Will we dream
together
of adventures
as yet unlived?
Will we kiss,
my lips to yours,
for a moment, a night,
for the rest of our lives?
Will we,
you and me,
do all the things?

If you knew
the nature of
my dreams,
      you might
      get scared
      or maybe
      keep me
      forever.

Whispers in the dark,
so I move ghostlike
through the house
trying to discover
the source of the words.
They remain elusive,
slipping into shadows,
silently drifting around
behind me.
The words follow
out of dreams
and nightmares
but they've lost
cohesion and distinction.
All I know is
someone who was here
continues to watch me.
Might as well
put on a good show.

A silver butterfly visited
and promised a fortune
for my soul.
She was first,
followed by a parade
of foxes
and ravens
and fairies
and fireflies,
and a magician
gorgeous as the night
in winter.
She promised nothing,
but she kissed me
under the moon
and said my soul
wasn't full yet,
but she'd come back.

Our love
is an ocean,
the tides
ever changing it,
always in motion,
sometimes calm
or tumultuous,
yet vast,
impossible
to ever see
the whole of,
different
every day
and subject
to the whims
of the moon.

How many times
must I tell you
I love you
    before I accept
    you don't
    love me?

This isn't a world
of absolutes
so you should
take the risk,
put everything
out in the open,
and trust
yourself
enough to know
now is the time.

Your superpower
and curse
has been
invisibility,
so no one sees you cry
and no one sees
when you're weak
but no one sees
when you're lonely
in the dark
or in the light
of day.

I recognize this
in you because
it's reflected in me.
I hear you,
in sunlight or moonshine
or shadow,
and when I look
in your direction
I see through
your shields
because they're
just like mine,
and I see you,
and what I see
is beautiful.

I will
    touch your cheeks
        with my fingers
    and lean close
        to hear your
        whispered secrets.
I will drink
    with you
        whatever we have
        on hand
    and dance
        with or without
        the moon's light.
And gently,
    I will kiss
        your throat
    and kiss your lips
    and kiss
        the pulse
        of your wrist.

If you let me.

And I think
    you'll let me.

Poison on your lips,
you warn me.
You're giving me
the choice,
to love or leave,
to live or die,
to dance with you
through the night
as my fever builds,
or to let
my fever climb
without
release.
You know already
the only choice
I can make,
but you
may not know
what to do
in the morning
when you discover
I've built up
an immunity
to your kind
of poison.

The end of a road
again
and there's no one
to tell me
I've done well,
no one saying
the next road
will be easier.
So I delude myself
and insist victory
is just
a few steps away.
I brave the hail
and swallow the storms
and dance to the echoes
of thunder
and I put
one more road
behind me
and start
on the next.

ACKNOWLEDGMENTS

It is impossible to write a poem without inspiration. Some inspirations may be brief, some life-changing, but those inspirations will always resonate through the words.

Readers will then attribute their own symbology and meaning and inspirations to the poems, which is precisely as it should be.

Inspiration can be a piece of art, a place, a thing someone has done, words someone has said, words no one has ever said, or a person.

Inspirations for the work in this book include Edgar Allan Poe, which should be obvious. Some of these poems could not have been written without some brief spark of thought or emotion from Ashley, Becky, Christina, Dawn, Eygló, Erin, Jezzy, Karen, Katie, Kristen, Kya, Linda, Miko, Upama, Veenu, Zelah, and others.

It is impossible to understate the inspiration, influence, and impact of Morgan.

As always, Sabine and the Rose Fairy continue to inspire.

ABOUT THE PROJECT AND AUTHOR

John Urbancik's business card proclaims him a Writer, Photographer, and Adventurer. Apparently, he is also a Poet, and this is his third such book.

Annabel Lee, in Shadow steals her name from an Edgar Allan Poe poem, but the story told through this narrative veers far from Poe's tale.

La Diosa del Fuego, more a collection of impressions than a narrative, nevertheless begins in one place and ends someplace else.

Romance and Miscellany shows other various and mysterious things that have spilled from Urbancik's mind, heart, and soul.

All of these poems were originally written by hand with a fountain pen.

ALSO BY JOHN URBANCIK

COLLECTIONS
Shadows, Legends & Secrets
Sound and Vision
Tales of the Fantastic and the Phantasmagoric
The Museum of Curiosities

POETRY
John the Revelator
Odyssey

NOVELLAS
A Game of Colors
The Rise and Fall of Babylon (with Brian Keene)
Wings of the Butterfly
House of Shadow and Ash
Necropolis
Quicksilver
Beneath Midnight
Zombies vs. Aliens vs. Robots vs. Cowboys vs.
Ninja vs. Investment Bankers vs. Green Berets
Colette and the Tiger
Madmen, Poets & Thieves
Clockwork Ravens
The Night Carnival
La Casa del Diablo

ALSO BY JOHN URBANCIK

NOVELS
Sins of Blood and Stone
Breath of the Moon
Once Upon a Time in Midnight
Stale Reality
The Corpse and the Girl from Miami
DarkWalker 1: Hunting Grounds
DarkWalker 2: Inferno
DarkWalker 3: The Deep City
DarkWalker 4: Armageddon
DarkWalker 5: Ghost Stories
DarkWalker 6: Other Realms
Choose Your Doom

NONFICTION
InkStained: On Creativity, Writing, and Art

INKSTAINS
Multiple volumes

www.ingramcontent.com/pod-product-compliance
Lightning Source LLC
Chambersburg PA
CBHW060234180626
46813CB00007B/3077